Fat P

Harriet Castor grew up in Warwickshire, where she went to a full-time dancing school. She has been writing stories for as long as she can remember, and wrote her first Puffin book, Fat Puss and Friends, at the age of twelve. After graduating from Cambridge University with a degree in History, she lived in Prague for a while, teaching English and getting lost on trams. Returning to Britain, she spent the next few years as an editor in children's publishing, but now writes full time.

Some other books by Harriet Castor

FAT PUSS ON WHEELS
FAT PUSS AND SLIM PUP

MILLY OF THE ROVERS
MILLY'S GOLDEN GOAL

HARRIET CASTOR

Fat Puss and Friends

Illustrated by Colin West

PUFFIN BOOKS

PUFFIN BOOKS

Published by the Penguin Group
Penguin Books Ltd, 80 Strand, London WC2R 0RL, England
Penguin Putnam Inc., 375 Hudson Street, New York, New York 10014, USA
Penguin Books Australia Ltd, 250 Camberwell Road, Camberwell, Victoria 3124, Australia
Penguin Books Canada Ltd, 10 Alcorn Avenue, Toronto, Ontario, Canada M4V 3B2
Penguin Books India (P) Ltd, 11 Community Centre, Panchsheel Park, New Delhi – 110 017, India
Penguin Books (NZ) Ltd, Cnr Rosedale and Airborne Roads, Albany, Auckland, New Zealand
Penguin Books (South Africa) (Pty) Ltd, 24 Sturdee Avenue, Rosebank 2196, South Africa

Penguin Books Ltd, Registered Offices: 80 Strand, London WC2R 0RL, England

www.penguin.com

First published by Viking Kestrel, 1984
Published in Puffin Books 1985

16

Text copyright © Harriet Castor, 1984
Illustrations copyright © Colin West, 1984
All rights reserved

Made and printed in England by Clays Ltd, St Ives plc

British Library Cataloguing in Publication Data
A CIP catalogue record for this book is available from
the British Library

ISBN 0–140–31658–2

CONTENTS

Fat Puss

Fat Puss was fat. He had little thin
arms, small flat feet, a very short tail
and an amazingly fat tummy.

Fat Puss was sad because all his friends teased him about being so fat. He was so enormous that there were lots of things he couldn't do.

Other cats could squeeze through
holes in fencing.

But Fat Puss couldn't.

Other cats could jump delicately onto thin bars.

But Fat Puss couldn't.

Other cats could walk through cat flaps.

But Fat Puss couldn't.

Other cats could hide in long grass.

But Fat Puss couldn't.

Other cats could walk about silently.
But Fat Puss couldn't.

One day when Fat Puss was feeling particularly sad, he decided to take a walk to cheer himself up. He plodded along, trying to think of something exciting to do.

Then, just as he came to the top of a hill, Fat Puss tripped over a stone!

And he rolled,

and he rolled,

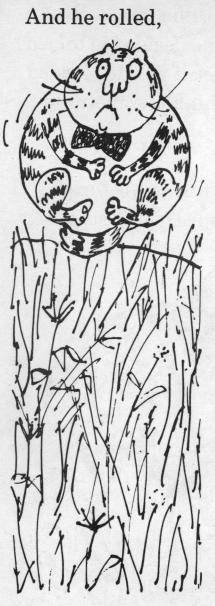

and he rolled all the way down the
hill, right to the bottom.

When Fat Puss finally stopped
rolling, he sat up. He had not been
hurt at all. In fact he had rather
enjoyed his unusual form of
travelling.

So when Fat Puss came to the next
hill, he rolled down that too. "Yippee!
This is fun!" he cried.

The next day Fat Puss told all his friends about his great new pastime.

All Fat Puss's friends tried rolling down hills, but because they had such long legs and long tails and were so thin and bony they couldn't roll properly and so got very bruised.

"Oh, we wish we could roll down hills like you, Fat Puss," they said.

Then Fat Puss was happy. He didn't mind that the other cats could do things that he couldn't because at last he had found an exciting thing that he and only he could do!

25

Fat Puss
Finds a Friend

Fat Puss was feeling miserable.
He had been rolling down hills so
much that his tummy was sore. So
he couldn't roll down hills any more
and he had nothing to do.

All Fat Puss's friends were busy chasing mice.

Fat Puss had tried to chase mice too, but he could never catch them because he couldn't run very fast.

Fat Puss felt so miserable that he sat down in a corner and cried.

Just then Fat Puss heard a little
voice.

"Hello," squeaked the little voice.
Fat Puss looked down. There, in front
of him, sat a small mouse. "Hello,"
said the mouse again.

Seeing the mouse made Fat Puss cry
even more. All the other cats could
have caught it but Fat Puss knew
that if he tried to catch the mouse it
would just run away so fast that he
wouldn't even be able to keep up with it.

"What's the matter?" asked the mouse. "I am so slow," sobbed Fat Puss, "that I can't even chase mice like all my friends do."

"I'm very glad about that," said the mouse. This made Fat Puss stop crying for a minute. "Why?" he asked. "Because we mice do not like being chased," replied the mouse.

"Really?" asked Fat Puss, who was very surprised at this.

"Yes," said the mouse, "we'd like cats a lot more if they didn't try to chase us."

"I never knew that," said Fat Puss, cheering up a little. "I suppose it's a good thing that I can't chase mice. Could you be my friend?"

"Of course," said the mouse, "as long
as you don't chase me. By the way,
my name's Terence."

"My name's Fat Puss," said Fat Puss.

Terence and Fat Puss became very good friends and Fat Puss was very pleased that he had found a companion.

Terence took Fat Puss to meet his wife, Jessica, and his children, Robert and Charlotte.

Fat Puss spent many sunny afternoons playing with the mouse family.

When all the other cats saw what fun
Fat Puss was having they said, "Oh,
we wish we could play with the mice
like you, Fat Puss. But because we
chased them, they won't be friends
with us."

Fat Puss was very, very pleased that he had not done as the other cats had done because now he had made four new friends.

Fat Puss
in Summer

One warm summer day the sun was
shining brightly. Fat Puss felt so hot
and thirsty that he sat down for a rest
under a tree.

He saw all the other cats drinking
from the pond, stretching their long
necks so that they could reach the
water without falling in.

Fat Puss wanted a drink very much, so he tried to copy them. He bent down and stretched his neck out as far as he could, but he couldn't reach the water.

He stretched a bit more,

and a bit more,

until all of a sudden,

SPLOSH!!! He tumbled into the pond,
head first.

"What shall I do?" thought Fat Puss.
"I can't swim!"

Soon Fat Puss found that he didn't
need to swim.

He was floating.

The other cats saw Fat Puss having
fun floating in the water. So they
tried to float too.

But they were so thin and bony that they couldn't float and they had to scramble quickly to the shore.

They climbed out looking wet and dripping. "We wish we could float in the pond like you, Fat Puss," they said.

Fat Puss was very glad that he could float in the pond. Now he could drink as much as he wanted to and have fun at the same time.

Fat Puss
Meets a Stranger

One day, Fat Puss went for a walk.

He came across a stream which he
had never seen before.

Fat Puss felt very hot, so he decided
to jump in the water and float around
for a while.

He enjoyed himself very much and he
was glad that he had come across this
new stream.

Suddenly, Fat Puss saw a brown, furry creature swimming towards him.

It raised its head and he saw that it
had very large teeth.

"Oh dear," thought Fat Puss. "What
shall I do? There is a brown, furry
monster with big, sharp teeth coming
towards me and it's going to eat me
up!"

Fat Puss could not swim, but he tried to scramble away. The creature was coming nearer and nearer.

Fat Puss closed his eyes and waited for the attack . . .

"Hello," said a friendly voice.

Fat Puss slowly opened his eyes and realized that it was the brown creature who had spoken. "H-hello," returned Fat Puss nervously.

"Don't be afraid," said the creature, "I won't harm you."

"You mean you're not going to eat me up?" asked Fat Puss.

"Why, no, of course not," chuckled the creature. "I don't eat animals, I only eat plants."

Fat Puss felt very relieved.

"My name is Humphrey. I am a beaver," said the creature.

"I am Fat Puss," said Fat Puss.

"Now we know each other better, would you like to come for a swim with me?" asked Humphrey.

"I'm afraid I can't swim," replied Fat Puss sadly. "I can only float."

"I shall teach you how to swim, then!"
exclaimed Humphrey.

"Thank you very much," said Fat
Puss.

Humphrey taught Fat Puss how to swim and they became very good friends.

Fat Puss introduced Humphrey to
Terence Mouse.

Fat Puss was very pleased to have found a new stream, learned to swim and to have made another nice new friend.

*Fat Puss
at Christmas*

One winter morning, Fat Puss went
for a walk.

He discovered that everything was
covered in something cold and white.

He didn't know what it was, so he
went to ask Terence Mouse.

"Oh, that's snow," said Terence.
"Don't be afraid of it, it's quite all
right." Fat Puss decided to ignore the
snow and do what he did every
morning: roll down a few hills.

Fat Puss found a hill and began to
roll.

But, as he rolled, the snow stuck to
him and then more snow stuck to this
snow, and soon he looked like a large
snowball.

"Oh dear," thought Fat Puss. "I can't see where I'm going. What shall I do?"

BUMP! It was too late for Fat Puss to do anything.

He had bumped into a little fir tree
and it had knocked all the snow off
him. But the tree had fallen down.

Fat Puss didn't like to leave the tree lying on the hill because somebody else might trip over it. He did not know what to do with it, so he picked it up and took it to show Terence.

"It's a Christmas tree!" said Terence.
"We must decorate it, and then we
can sing carols around it on
Christmas Day."

"Oh, what a lovely idea!" exclaimed
Fat Puss.

Terence collected fir cones and old leaves and conkers left over from autumn.

Terence's children, Robert and Charlotte, painted them bright colours.

Terence's wife, Jessica, collected milk bottle tops that untidy people had dropped.

Then Fat Puss hung all the things on his tree until it looked gay and pretty.

Then, on Christmas Day, Fat Puss and the Mouse family all had fun singing carols around their own Christmas tree. And Humphrey the beaver joined them for tea.

The End.

Also in Young Puffin

FAT PUSS ON WHEELS

Harriet Castor

Fat Puss has fun!

Fat Puss, the roly-poly cat, is up to his old tricks, and has no end of adventures with his friends the Mouse family and Humphrey Beaver. He goes flying, is the hero of the football match, and roller-skates into the river!

Join Fat Puss in his funny and surprising escapades!

READ MORE IN PUFFIN

For children of all ages, Puffin represents quality and variety – the very best in publishing today around the world.

For complete information about books available from Puffin – and Penguin – and how to order them, contact us at the appropriate address below. Please note that for copyright reasons the selection of books varies from country to country.

On the world wide web: www.penguin.co.uk

In the United Kingdom: Please write to *Dept. EP, Penguin Books Ltd, Bath Road, Harmondsworth, West Drayton, Middlesex UB7 ODA*
Schools Line in the UK: Please write to

In the United States: Please write to *Consumer Sales, Penguin USA, P.O. Box 999, Dept. 17109, Bergenfield, New Jersey 07621-0120.* VISA and MasterCard holders call 1-800-253-6476 to order Penguin titles

In Canada: Please write to *Penguin Books Canada Ltd, 10 Alcorn Avenue, Suite 300, Toronto, Ontario M4V 3B2*

In Australia: Please write to *Penguin Books Australia Ltd, P.O. Box 257, Ringwood, Victoria 3134*

In New Zealand: Please write to *Penguin Books (NZ) Ltd, Private Bag 102902, North Shore Mail Centre, Auckland 10*

In India: Please write to *Penguin Books India Pvt Ltd, 706 Eros Apartments, 56 Nehru Place, New Delhi 110 019*

In the Netherlands: Please write to *Penguin Books Netherlands bv, Postbus 3507, NL-1001 AH Amsterdam*

In Germany: Please write to *Penguin Books Deutschland GmbH, Metzlerstrasse 26, 60594 Frankfurt am Main*

In Spain: Please write to *Penguin Books S. A., Bravo Murillo 19, 1° B, 28015 Madrid*

In Italy: Please write to *Penguin Italia s.r.l., Via Felice Casati 20, I–20124 Milano*

In France: Please write to *Penguin France S. A., 17 rue Lejeune, F–31000 Toulouse*

In Japan: Please write to *Penguin Books Japan, Ishikiribashi Building, 2–5–4, Suido, Bunkyo-ku, Tokyo 112*

In South Africa: Please write to *Longman Penguin Southern Africa (Pty) Ltd, Private Bag X08, Bertsham 2013*